DIXIE PUBLIC SCHOOL

Holt, Rinehart and Winston, Inc.

Holt, Rinehart and Winston, London, Sydney

New York, Toronto,

Copyright © 1970
by Holt, Rinehart and Winston, Inc.
Published simultaneously in Canada
Printed in the United States of America
Library of Congress Catalog Card Number: 79-109191
All rights reserved. Permission must be secured
for broadcasting, tape recording,
mechanically duplicating or reproducing
in any way any part of this book
for any purpose. Permission

SBN: 03-084582-3

© Bill Martin 25tant Reader

WHEN it RAINS..
IT RAINS

by Bill Martin, Jr.
with pictures by Emanuele Luzzati

When it rains, it rains.

When it snows, it snows.

When it fogs, it fogs.

When it blows,

it

blows.

When it's hot, it's hot.

When it's cold, it's cold.

When you're young, you're young.

When you're old, you're old.

When I'm merry, I'm merry.

When I'm sad, I'm sad.

When I'm good, I'm good.

But when I'm bad...

I'm perfectly **horri-**

...ble.